NARWHAL
BACK
AT
1:00

Is
for
Salad

To Cindy

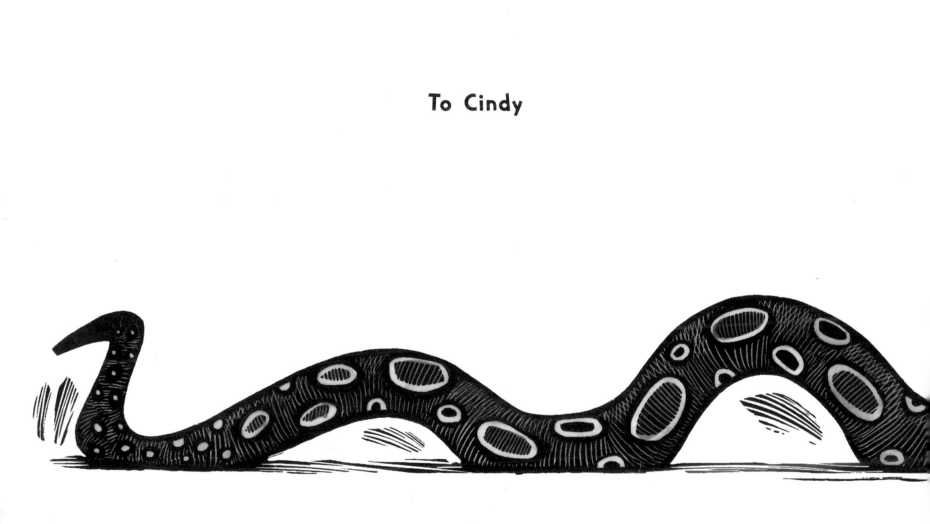

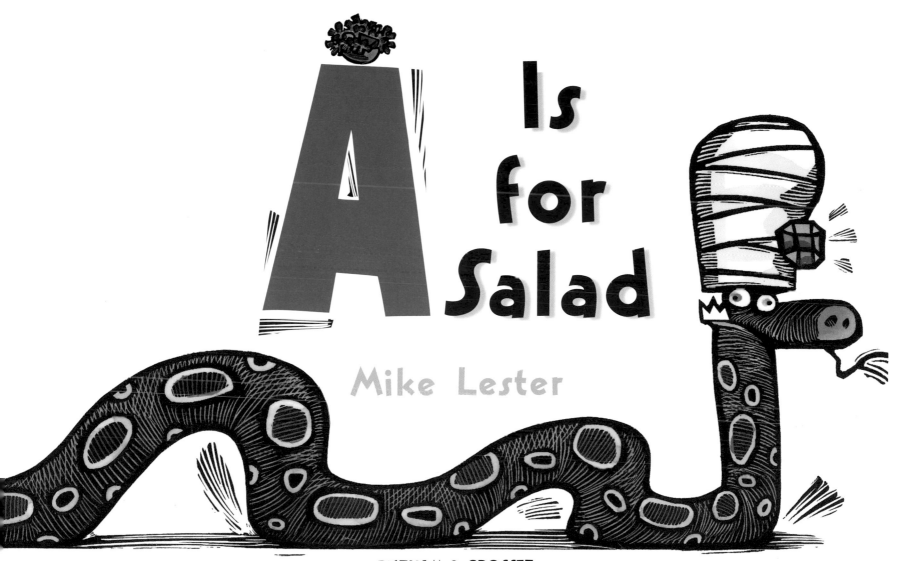

A Is for Salad

Mike Lester

PUTNAM & GROSSET
New York

A

is for **salad**.

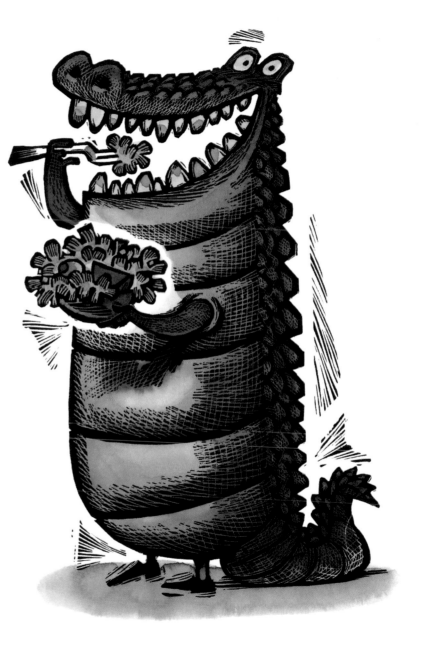

is for **Viking.**

C

is for
hot dog.

D is for remote control
...isn't it?

E is for **pajamas.**

F

is for **soup.**

G

is for
soccer.

H

is for

pizza

...I think.

I is for **pancakes.**

J is for **hats.**

K

is for

doctor.

L

is for

hair dryer.

M

is for
cowboy
boots.

O

is for
bow ties

and

P is for

roller skates.

I'm sure of that.

I can't figure out what

is for.
Can you?

R

is for
bowling.

S

is for

tennis.

T is for polka-dotted underpants.

U is for "Go Fish!".

V is for **wiggly worm.**

W

is for
birthday
cake.

and

are **not** important letters. Never use them.

And

Z

is for...

The End.

Published by The Putnam & Grosset Group,
a division of Penguin Putnam Books for Young Readers, New York.
Published simultaneously in Canada. Printed in Singapore.

Library of Congress Cataloging-in-Publication Data

Lester, Mike.
A is for salad / Mike Lester.   p.   cm.
Summary: Each letter of the alphabet is presented
in an unusual way, such as: "A is for salad" showing
an alligator eating a bowl of greens.
[1. Alphabet.] I. Title.
PZ7.L562951s
1999   [E]—dc21   99-20900   CIP
ISBN 0-399-23388-1   C D E F G H I J

A is also for alligator.

B is also for beaver.

C is also for cat.

D is also for duck.

I is also for iguana.

J is also for jellyfish.

K is also for kangaroo.

L is also for lion.

R is also for rabbit.

S is also for snake.

T is also for tiger.

U is also for unicorn.